To Carys,

for taking one step...

First published 2003 by Walker Books Ltd
87 Vauxhall Walk, London SE11 5HJ

10 9 8 7 6 5 4 3 2 1

This book had been typeset in Throhand Ink Roman

Printed in Italy

British Library Cataloguing in Publication Data:
a catalogue record for this book is
available from the British Library

ISBN 0-7445-9286-0

Simon James

one step...

Little
One
Step

WALKER BOOKS
AND SUBSIDIARIES
LONDON · BOSTON · SYDNEY

"We're lost!" said
the eldest duckling.

"It won't be far,"
said the middle one.

"I want my mama,"
whispered the little one.

"My legs feel all wobbly."

"Tell you what," said his eldest brother.
"Have you tried doing One Step?"
"What's that?" said the little one.

"Watch carefully," said
his brother. "Just lift
one foot like this ...

and say 'one'."
"One," said the little one.

"Then put it down in front
and say 'step!'"
"Step," said the little one.

"Then start again with the
other foot," said his brother.
"Can I practise for a bit?"
said the little one.

"I think you've got it!" said his eldest brother.
"We'll call you Little One Step from now on,"
said his middle brother.

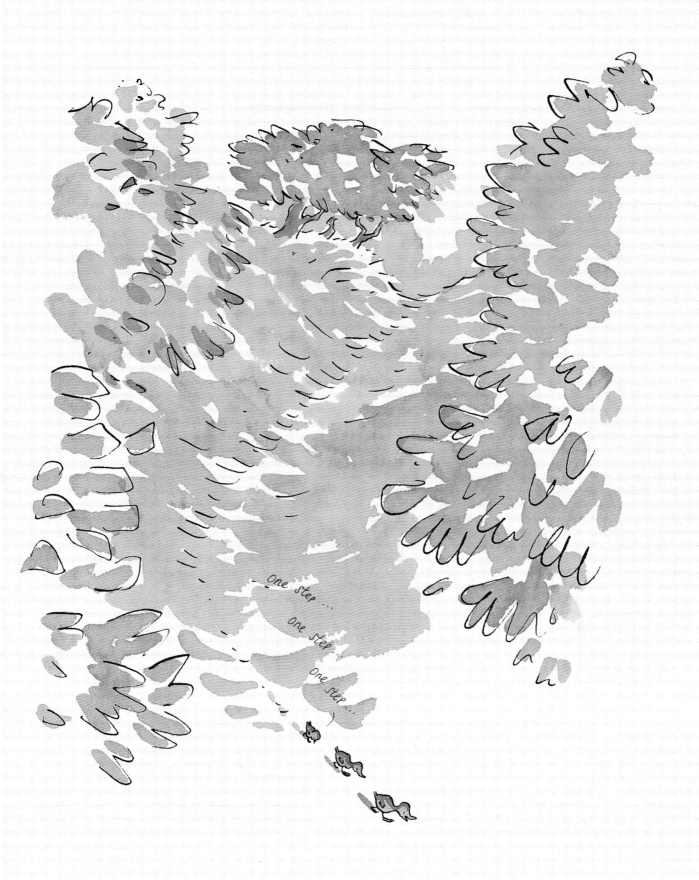

"One step ... one step ..."
said Little One Step,
until ...

he looked up at the tall trees.

"It's no good," he said.
"My legs feel all wobbly again."

"Did you forget to do One Step?"
said his eldest brother.

"Oh yes, I suppose I did,"
said Little One Step.

"I'll try again.
One ...

step. There!"
he said.

"One step ... one step ..."
said Little One Step.

At last they reached
a clearing.
The river was down below.
"If we cut across the field
we'll be home," said the
middle one.

"I can't walk all that way,"
said Little One Step.
"I want my mama!"
"We're nearly there,"
said his eldest brother.
"Just do One Step."

"One step ... one step ...

one step!" said Little One Step.

Little One Step marched
through the field ...

past his brothers ...

through the undergrowth ...

into a clearing.

"Mama! It's you!" shouted Little One Step.
"My baby!" said Mama.

"My boys!" said Mama.

"Hello, Mama," said the brothers.

"We're so glad to see you!"

Little One Step led them all
down to the river.

At the water's edge he stopped.

"Mama, do you know my
new name?" he asked.

one step...

"Little One Step!" said Little One Step,
and in he went.